This book is a work of fiction. Any references to historical events, real people, or real places are used fictitiously. Other names, characters, places, and events are products of the author's imagination, and any resemblance to actual events or places or persons, living or dead, is entirely coincidental.

LITTLE SIMON
An imprint of Simon & Schuster Children's Publishing Division · 1230 Avenue of the Americas, New York, New York 10020 · First Little Simon hardcover edition May 2015 · For information about special discounts for bulk purchases, please contact Simon & Schuster Special Sales at 1-866-506-1949 or business@simonandschuster.com. The Simon & Schuster Speakers Bureau can bring authors to your live event. For more information or to book an event contact the Simon & Schuster Speakers Bureau at 1-866-248-3049 or visit our website at www.simonspeakers.com.
Designed by Laura Roode. The text of this book was set in Usherwood.
Manufactured in the United States of America 0415 FFG
10 9 8 7 6 5 4 3 2 1
Library of Congress Cataloging-in-Publication Data
Green, Poppy. Forget-Me-Not Lake / by Poppy Green ; illustrated by Jennifer A. Bell. — First edition. pages cm. — (The adventures of Sophie Mouse ; #3)
Summary: Sophie Mouse wants to prove how wonderful mice are for a school project she is doing with her brother, Winston, but starts to have doubts when, even with Hattie and Owen's help, she is unable to learn to swim.
[1. Mice—Fiction. 2. Ability—Fiction. 3. Swimming—Fiction. 4. Frogs—Fiction. 5. Snakes—Fiction.] I. Bell, Jennifer (Jennifer A.), 1977- illustrator. II. Title.
PZ7.G82616For 2015 [E]—dc23 2014026233
ISBN 978-1-4814-3000-5 (hc)
ISBN 978-1-4814-2999-3 (pbk)
ISBN 978-1-4814-3002-9 (eBook)

the adventures of

SOPHIE MOUSE

3

Forget-Me-Not Lake

By Poppy Green • Illustrated by Jennifer A. Bell

LITTLE SIMON
New York London Toronto Sydney New Delhi

Contents

chapter 1

Mouse Life

Sophie Mouse skipped around the toadstool table. She added a carved-twig spoon to each of the four place settings.

"Napkin on the *left*, Winston," she told her little brother as they set the table for dinner. "Spoon on the right."

"Okay, Sophie," replied Winston. "Wait. Which side is left again?"

Sophie tried to be patient as she reminded him. She took a deep breath. Her nose twitched. Her whiskers quivered with glee. Delicious aromas filled the Mouse family's house in the hollow of a big oak tree.

Sophie's father, George Mouse, was at the stove. He was stirring a big pot of radish soup.

Sophie's mother, Lily Mouse, peeked into the oven. She was trying out a new recipe—clover and juniper berry cake.

Sophie came over to look at the

cake too. "We should *probably* try it before you add it to the bakery menu." She smiled sweetly at her mother. "Don't you think?"

Lily Mouse owned the only bakery in Pine Needle Grove. She was known for making the most delicious cakes and pastries—often with unexpected ingredients.

Lily Mouse smiled back at Sophie. "Yes, of course," she said. "We will all have a test piece—*after* dinner!"

Before long, the soup was ready. George Mouse ladled it into walnut-shell bowls. Then all four mice sat down for Friday night dinner.

As they slurped their soup, Sophie and Winston had lots to tell about their week at school. Mrs. Wise, their teacher at Silverlake Elementary, had assigned the students a fun project.

"We have to prepare a presentation about our own species," Sophie

explained. "The frog students will talk about frogs. The birds will talk about birds. And the mice will talk about mice. Next week, we'll each give our presentations to the class. It's to help us learn more about one another."

Winston's eyes were wide with excitement. "And since we're both mice, Sophie and I get to work together!" he added.

Winston was six years old. It was the first year he was old enough to come to school at the schoolhouse.

"Winston suggested we say that mice are fast and can scurry places quickly," Sophie pointed out.

"And Sophie said we should talk about how we're small and can fit into tiny spaces," Winston added.

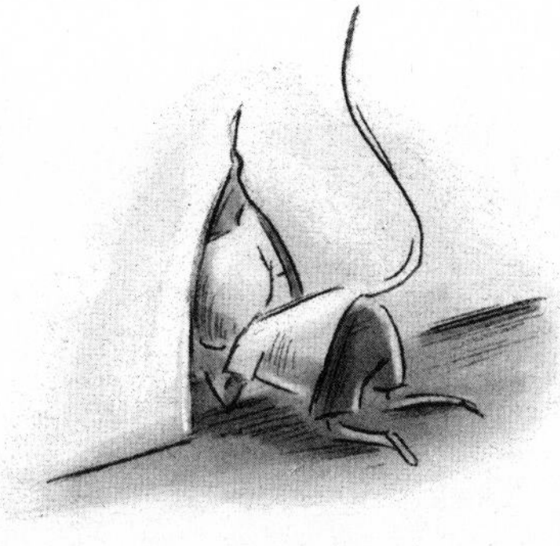

George Mouse smiled. "Very true," he said. "Can you think of other things we mice are good at?"

Sophie and Winston thought it over. Winston put his elbow on the table and rested his chin in his hand. Sophie gazed out the window, puzzling over the question.

But neither one could think of anything. Something was distracting them. They both sniffed the air.

Their whiskers twitched.

They looked at each other. Then they shouted it out together.

"The cake is ready!"

chapter 2

A Sunny Saturday

Sophie sat up in bed. She yawned and stretched. Sun streamed in through the knothole window.

"A perfect day to play at the lake!" she cried. She and her friends Hattie and Owen had made plans. They were going to meet at Forget-Me-Not Lake after breakfast.

Sophie jumped out of bed and

hurried to get dressed. As she pulled on her jumper, she paused. Her latest painting sat just where she'd left it on her easel. It was of a beautiful marigold she had seen the other day.

"Maybe this evening I'll paint a scene of our day at the lake," Sophie said to herself. She couldn't wait to use her new color, cornflower blue. She'd made it by grinding up bright-blue cornflower petals. "With a touch of green it could be just right for painting the water!"

Sophie ran downstairs. Winston and Mrs. Mouse were nibbling on freshly baked peach and poppy seed muffins.

Sophie reminded her mom that she was running off to meet Hattie and Owen.

"Okay," said Mrs. Mouse. "But have some breakfast first!"

Sophie grabbed a muffin. Then she took two more for Hattie and Owen. She wrapped them up in a linen napkin and tied it into a bundle.

"Your father is working today," Mrs. Mouse said. Mr. Mouse was the town architect. He was overseeing the construction of a rabbit's new house. "Winston will come with me to the bakery. Come find us there if you need anything.

And be home in time for dinner!"

"I will!" Sophie cried. She grabbed the napkin bundle and headed for the door. Then she stopped and turned. "And Winston, let's work on our project tonight!"

She heard Winston cheer as she headed out into the fresh air.

Forget-Me-Not Lake was a pretty long walk from Sophie's house. She headed toward town, then turned off onto the path that led to the lake. Along the way, she passed Oak Hollow Theater. Sophie had gone there once to see a play. The audience sat on carved-out logs that were arranged in rows on a slight

slope. The stage was at the bottom. In that log, there were several large holes. When the setting sun hit at just the right angle, it streamed through the holes and made spotlights that lit up the stage. Sophie thought it was beautiful.

Finally, the path came out of the woods. Sophie was standing on the bank of a big, glistening lake. It was surrounded by forget-me-nots—tiny blue flowers with yellow centers

that bloomed in bunches on little green stems. That's why it was called Forget-Me-Not Lake.

Very close by, a voice made Sophie jump. "Finally! We were wondering

when you'd get here!"

Sophie turned. Her friend Owen was hanging from a tree. His tail was wound around a low branch.

"Owen! You startled me!" Sophie cried. Then she laughed. "You're too good at sneaking up on me."

"Sorry," said Owen. "I can't help it. That's just how we snakes are, I guess."

His eyes lit up. “Hey! I should add that to my presentation for school!”

Sophie looked around. “Where’s Hattie?” she asked.

Owen looked around too. “Huh,” he said. “She was just here. Hattie! HAT-tie!”

There was no answer.

Sophie tried. “HAT-TIE! Where are you?” She turned to Owen. “Where could she have gone?”

chapter 3

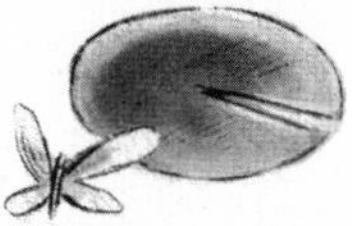

Green with Frog Envy

SPLASH!

Suddenly, in a flash of green, Hattie broke the still surface of the water. She leaped out of the lake and landed right at Sophie's side. Water droplets flew off of her and onto Sophie.

"Whoa!" Sophie cried. "Good underwater hiding place!"

"Did I surprise you?" Hattie asked hopefully. Usually it was Sophie or Owen who won at hide-and-seek.

Sophie nodded and unwrapped her napkin bundle. "I brought treats from my mom," she said.

"Yum!" exclaimed Owen.

The three friends climbed onto a large rock that was sitting in the shallow water. They sat down and nibbled muffins while they talked.

They had just been together the day before at school. But they never ran out of things they *had* to tell one another.

"This morning, a groundhog popped up from under our kitchen floor!" Owen shared. "He said he must have taken a wrong turn. He promised to fix the hole. But you should have seen my mom's face!"

Hattie and Sophie giggled.

Then Hattie shared her exciting news. “My parents are going out tonight. And Lydie’s going to watch me!” Lydie was Hattie’s big sister. “She said she’d show me how to make braided ribbon-grass bracelets!”

Soon, the friends' talk turned to the school project. "I've started working on mine," Owen said. "But I can't think of many cool things that snakes can do."

Sophie and Hattie looked at Owen as if he were crazy. "What do you mean?" said Hattie. "You can reach way up high and way down low with your tail, for one thing."

"Yeah!" Sophie agreed. "Remember how you saved me? That time I fell into that hole in the meadow? You lowered your tail all the way down so I could climb out!"

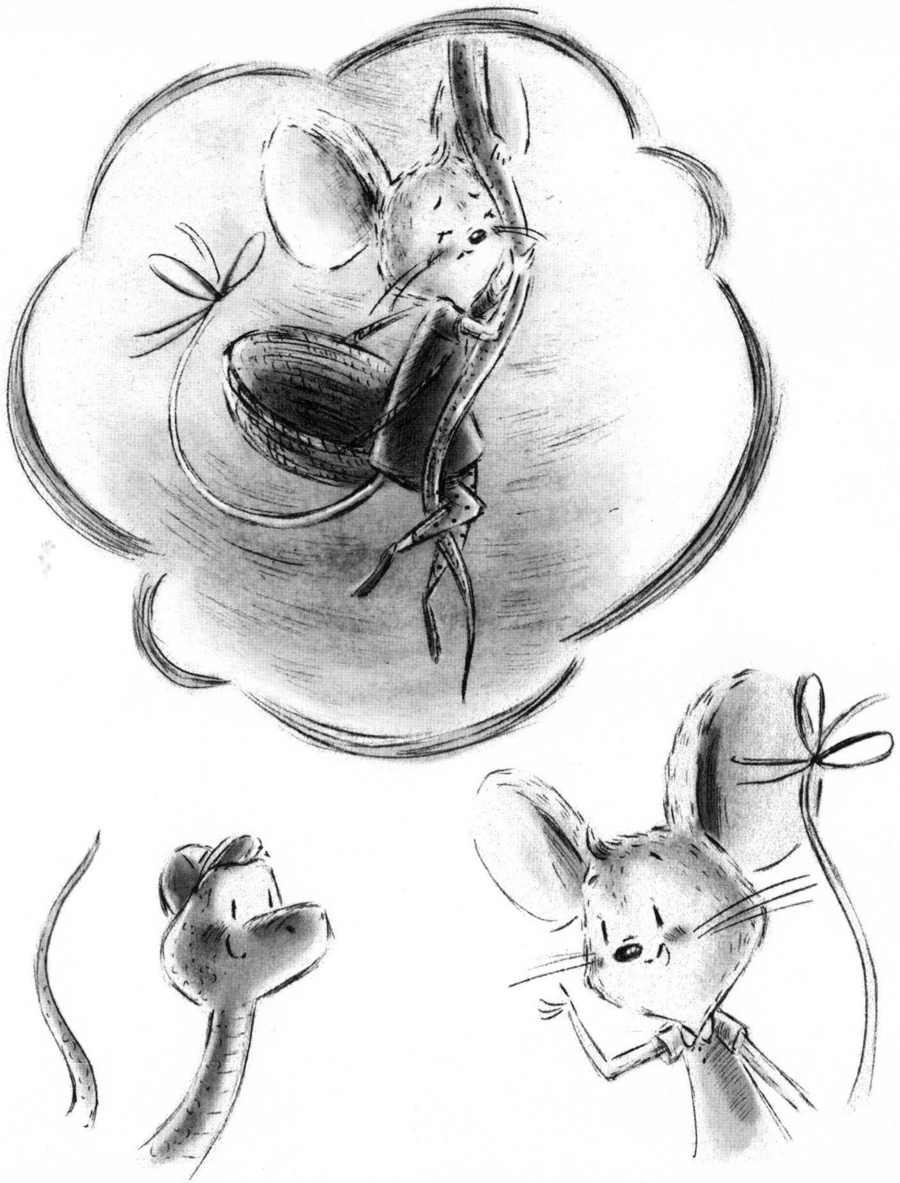

Owen smiled proudly. "That's true," he said, remembering. "Oh! And I just thought of something else!"

Owen dove into the water—*splash!*—and stayed under.

"What is he doing?" Sophie asked.

"I have no idea. Oh, wait!" cried

Hattie, pointing. "Look at all those patterns on the surface! Owen is making them!"

Sophie watched the *S*-shaped wavelets ripple across the water, catching glints of sunlight. It was so beautiful!

Owen came up at last, and Sophie and Hattie clapped.

"I wish *I* could do that!" said Hattie wistfully. "Being a frog isn't all that fun, I guess."

Sophie gasped. "What?!" she said.

"But Hattie," Owen said, "you can hop farther than anyone!"

Hattie seemed to think about it for a minute. Then she got a twinkle in her eye. She hopped off the rock onto a lily pad. She bounced to another, and another. Finally, she hopped into the air, flipped, and did a swan dive into the water.

When she came up from underwater, Sophie and Owen cheered.

"Amazing!" Sophie called.

"Wow!" Owen cried.

Sophie felt it was her turn now. "Winston and I have started making a list of things mice can do," she

said. Which cool thing should she demonstrate for her friends? Sophie ran through the list in her mind.

But as she did, Sophie's heart sank. Scurrying quickly and fitting into small spaces didn't seem so

interesting. Sophie kind of wished *she* could make cool water patterns or do perfect dives into the lake. But Sophie had never learned how to swim.

For the first time since Mrs. Wise gave the assignment, Sophie felt a

pang of doubt. She didn't say it out loud. She knew her friends would say she was being silly. But Sophie wondered. . . .

Was being a *mouse* the least exciting of all?

chapter 4

odd one out

Just then, a flock of ducks flew by. Sophie, Hattie, and Owen were distracted, watching them splash down on the far side of the lake.

Lucky ducks, thought Sophie. *They can swim* and *fly!*

"So," said Hattie, "what should we do today?"

Sophie tried to push her doubts

out of her mind. After all, it was a sunny Saturday in Silverlake Forest. The friends had nothing to do all day except have fun.

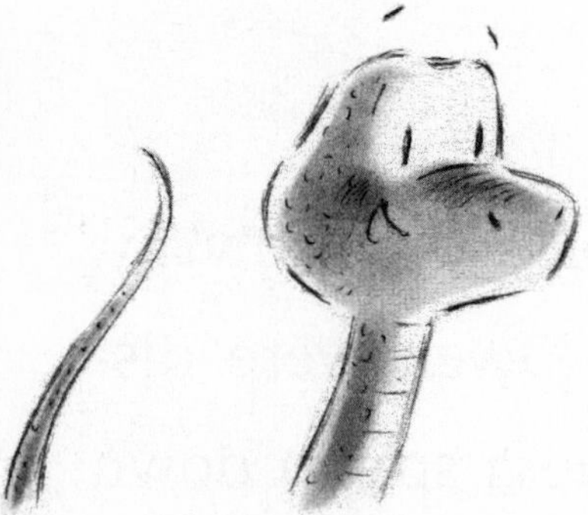

"Ooh!" said Owen excitedly. "We could swim across the lake. We could race!"

"Or we could judge each other's diving!" Hattie suggested.

Sophie didn't say anything. She didn't want to spoil their fun. But she couldn't do either one of those things.

It didn't take long for Hattie to realize it too. "Wait. That's no fun," said Hattie. "Let's think of something all three of us can do together."

Sophie smiled. She loved how Hattie could almost always tell what she was thinking.

"How about tag?" said Owen.

Sophie shrugged. Hattie did too. They played tag a lot at school during recess.

"Lily pad hopping?" Sophie said. She and Hattie did that a bunch when it was just the two of them at the lake. Sophie rode on Hattie's

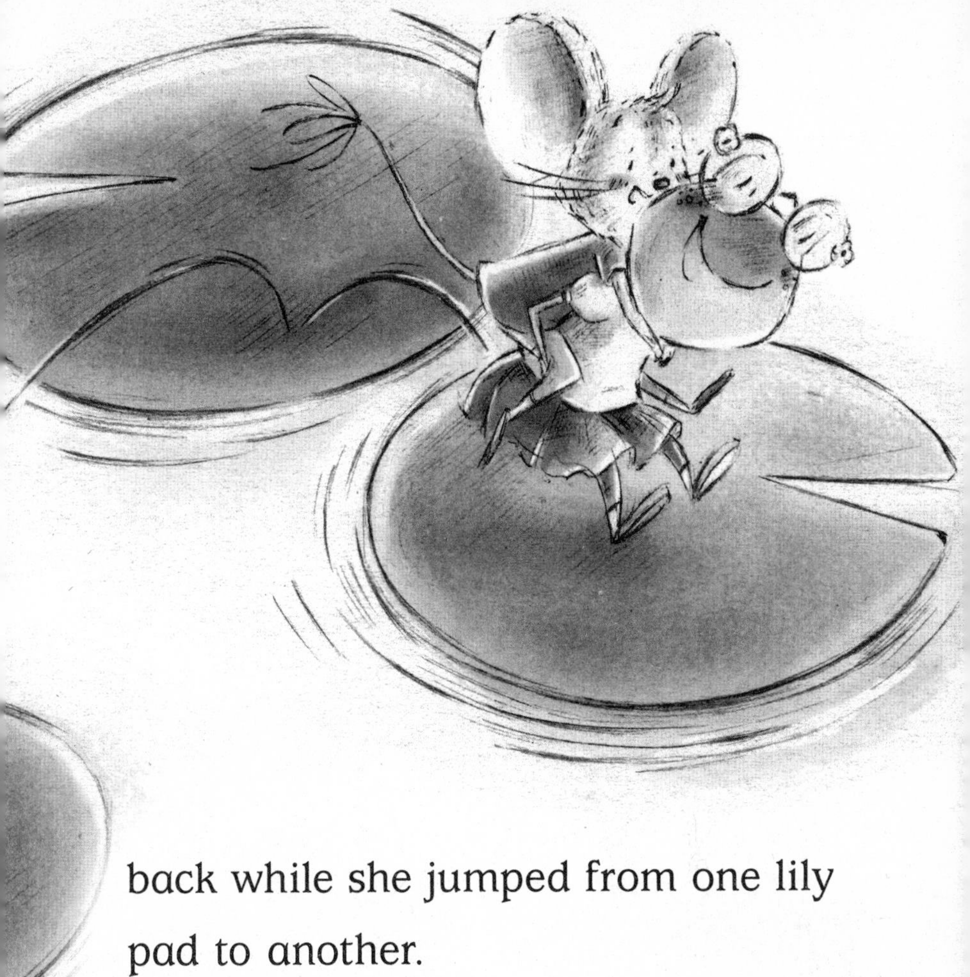

back while she jumped from one lily pad to another.

But Hattie couldn't carry Owen and Sophie at the same time. Plus Sophie could tell it wasn't what her friends *really* wanted to do.

"You know what?" said Sophie at last. "You two play in the water. I'll go pick some flowers to use for paint."

Hattie squinted at Sophie. "I don't know," she said uncertainly.

"Are you sure?" Owen asked.

Sophie nodded. "Yes, it's really okay!" she replied. And she meant it. It would be good to gather a bunch of paint supplies. She was running low at home.

Plus, thought Sophie, *when Hattie and Owen are done in the water, we'll do something else—all together.*

So Sophie wandered along the shore of the lake. She picked buttercups to use to make buttercup yellow paint. She found pink clover flowers to make clover pink.

She glanced over at the lake. Hattie and Owen were splashing each other.

Sophie wandered some more. She picked some tiny wild strawberries for making berry, berry red.

Hattie's voice and Owen's laugh drifted over on the breeze. Sophie looked their way to see them lining up to race across the lake.

Soon Sophie had ingredients for making at least ten different colors. She sat down on the shore of the lake and watched Hattie and Owen play. They were bobbing up for air. Then they were returning underwater to speak in bubble-talk.

The minutes dragged by. Sophie tried hard not to feel left out. After

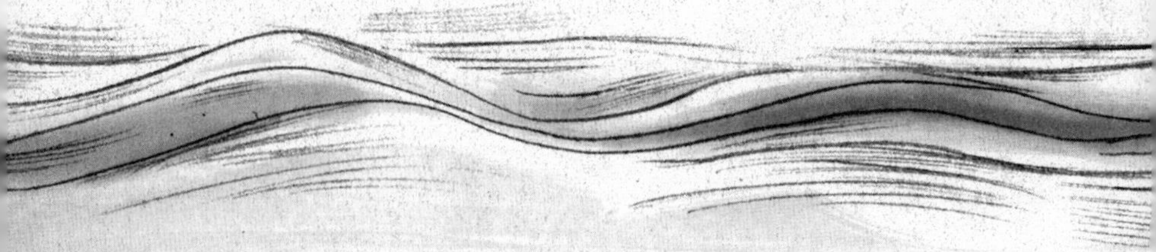

all, she had told them to go ahead and play in the water. She just didn't think they'd do it for *so long*.

Sophie sighed. *Here we are at Forget-Me-*Not *Lake,* she thought. *So why does it feel like my friends have forgotten me?*

chapter 5

Library Quest

The rest of Sophie's day with her friends was much better. They skipped rocks on the water. They found ripe blackberries to snack on. They played leap frog along the path back to town.

Even so, when Sophie got home, she didn't feel like working on the school project. "We'll do it tomorrow," she told Winston, who met her at the front door.

The next morning, Sophie woke up in a better mood. It helped that what woke her was the scent of her mother's rosemary-mint scones wafting upstairs.

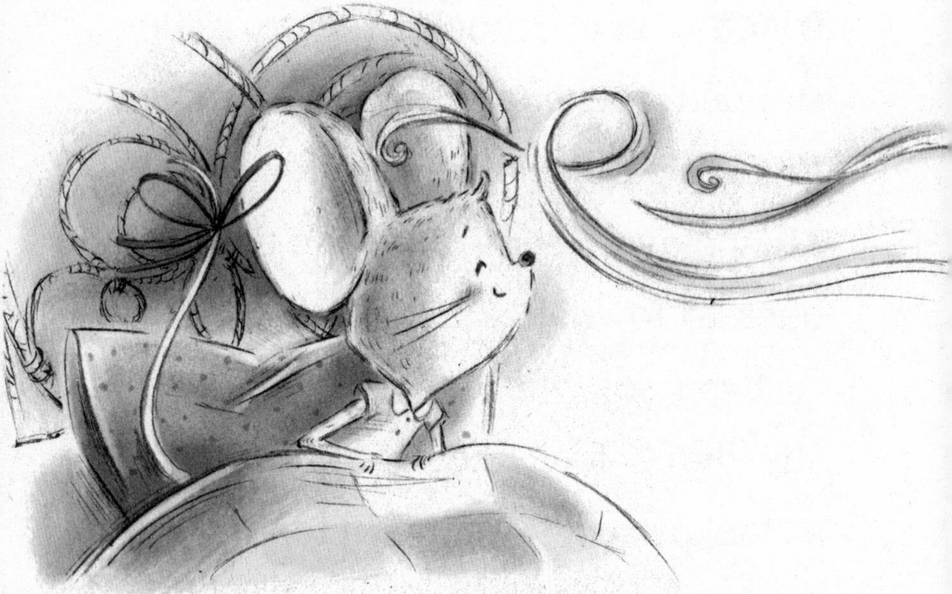

She also woke up with an idea. She and Winston could go to the library later. Maybe they'd find books with some *really* fascinating facts about mice!

First the siblings had to do their morning chores. Sophie swept out the bedrooms and hung the wet laundry to dry. Winston gathered dandelion greens for that night's salad and

counted how many vegetables were left in the root cellar. Lily Mouse said it was good counting practice.

When they were finished, they walked into town with their mother. She headed for the bakery while Sophie and Winston went off to the library. "Come have a snack when you're done!" she called after them.

The library was the oldest and biggest building in town. Inside,

wooden shelves of books rose up to the ceiling. Tall ladders on wheels helped the librarians reach the top shelves.

Sophie and Winston went right to the young readers' section in the back. They saw two of their friends sitting at a tree-stump table: their rabbit classmates, Ben and his little brother, James.

Sophie said hello and Winston hurried to James's side. The two younger siblings were the same age. They usually sat next to each other at school.

"Are you here working on your project too?" Winston asked.

James nodded. He pointed to a picture in the book he was reading.

"Did you know that we rabbits can swivel our eyes *all the way around*?!" James asked.

"So we can see behind us without turning our heads," Ben added.

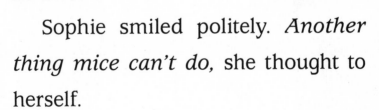

Winston's jaw dropped. "That is so cool!" he cried in awe.

Sophie smiled politely. *Another thing mice can't do,* she thought to herself.

Sophie wandered off to find the books on mice. At the end of a row of shelves, she found Malcolm Mole reading in a comfy corner.

"Hey, Sophie!" he said. "Did you know moles can dig up to eighteen feet in one hour?"

Sophie shook her head. "I did not know that," she said. She knew for

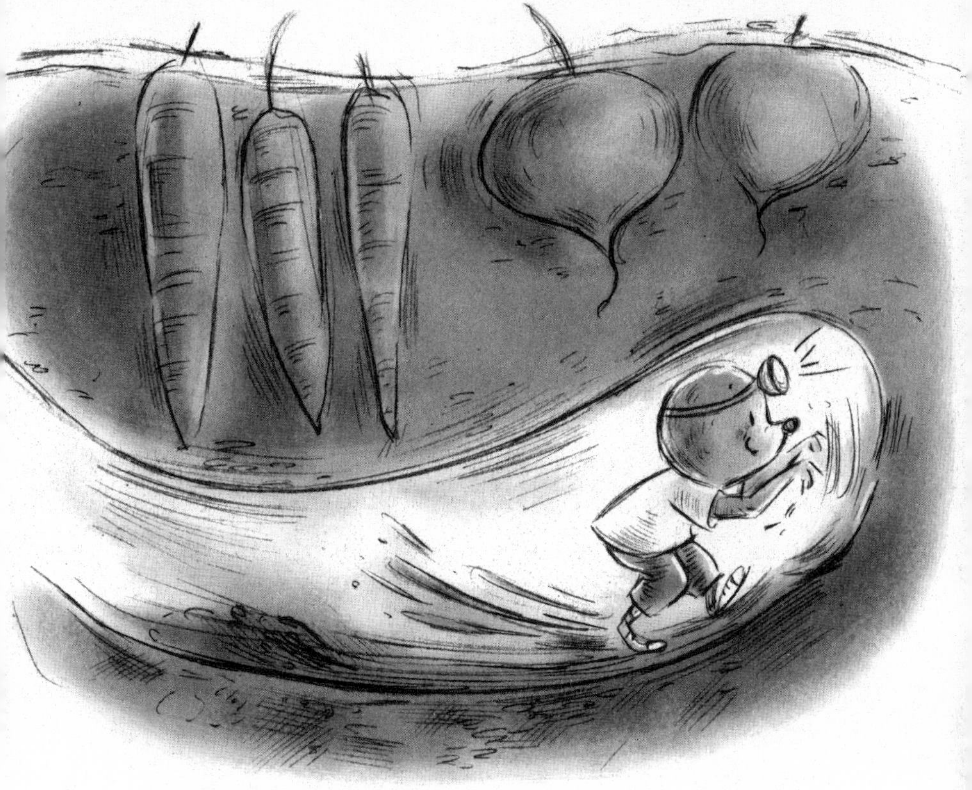

sure that mice couldn't do that either.

In front of the section of animal books, Sophie found Piper, her hummingbird friend. She was hovering in front of the hummingbird books.

"Sophie, isn't this just the best project?" Piper said. "I didn't know that we're the only birds that can fly backward!"

Sophie gulped. It seemed like everyone in class had something exciting to share in their presentation.

She scanned the shelves for mouse

books. With a sigh of relief, she found them. They were right between the books on mountain lions and musk oxen.

Then Sophie had a terrible thought: What if they didn't have any amazing mouse facts in them after all?

chapter 6

The Swim Lesson

Sophie found five books about mice. She carried the stack to an empty table. Then she sat down and started flipping through them.

She read about what mice liked to eat.

Sophie shrugged. "Boring," she said.

She read about mice and climbing.

Everyone knows that, she thought. Then she turned the page.

Sophie's heart was racing with excitement—and nervousness. She had never met a swimming mouse before! She bet most of her classmates hadn't either.

What if she, Sophie Mouse, could learn to swim? *That* would be an exciting tidbit for the presentation! This book made it sound like something she *could* do—if she had the courage to try.

"Okay!" said Hattie. "Let's review our water safety rules!"

Sophie, Hattie, and Owen were back at Forget-Me-Not Lake. Sophie

had asked her friends to give her a swim lesson. But now . . . Sophie was having second thoughts.

"First, we'll all stay in the shallow

water," Hattie was saying. "Second, we must stick together. Third, either Owen or I will have our eyes on Sophie whenever she is trying to swim."

"Agreed!" said Owen.

Sophie took a deep breath. *I can do this,* she told herself, and tried to believe it.

With her friends on either side of her, Sophie slowly waded

into the lake. It was cool on her legs as she went deeper and deeper.

When Sophie was waist deep, Hattie stopped. "This is good," she said. "Let's get you used to this depth."

Sophie smiled uncertainly. The water felt really . . . *wet*. A shiver went up her spine.

"Now let's try floating." Hattie suggested.

Hattie demonstrated. She lay back on the surface of the water. She stretched her arms and legs out to the sides and—*ta-da*!

Owen was also floating on the

surface. "The water holds us up," said Owen.

Doubt crept into Sophie's mind. "Hmm. That looks tricky," she said.

Hattie stood up. "Don't worry," she said. "We'll help you."

Sophie's friends stood close on

either side of her. They held on to her as she started to lie back into the water. “Good,” said Hattie. “We’ve got you. Tilt your head waaaaay back.”

Sophie got about halfway there. But she just couldn’t lie all the way back. It didn’t feel natural. Plus, she was worried about getting water in her ears!

Sophie jumped up suddenly. "Um, I'm not sure I can do that . . . yet," she said.

"That's okay!" said Hattie. "We'll try something else."

They showed Sophie how they could dunk their heads underwater

and try to sit on the bottom of the lake. “Take a deep breath,” said Owen.

“And hold it!” added Hattie.

“And just sit down in the water!” finished Owen.

Hattie and Owen did it. They made it look so easy!

Sophie's friends popped up. Now it was her turn. She took a deep breath and held it. She got ready to go under and . . .

She couldn't do it.

"How about just getting wet up to your neck?" Owen said.

Sophie nodded. "One . . . two . . . three . . . ," she counted.

Then she froze. Her knees wouldn't bend.

Sophie's shoulders drooped. "Oh," she groaned, feeling frustrated. "This isn't going to work. Thanks for trying, you guys." She turned and leaped out of the lake.

"Sophie, wait!" Hattie called after her.

"Come back!" cried Owen.

But Sophie hit dry land and ran all the way home.

chapter 7

A Sophie-Size Surprise

At home Sophie's dad was reading a book in the living room. She changed out of her swimsuit and flopped onto her bed.

By then, Sophie was all out of tears. When George Mouse knocked to see if she was okay, she said she was fine.

"I'm just painting," Sophie called

to him. But really, she lay there, staring at the ceiling. She was painting a picture in her *mind*.

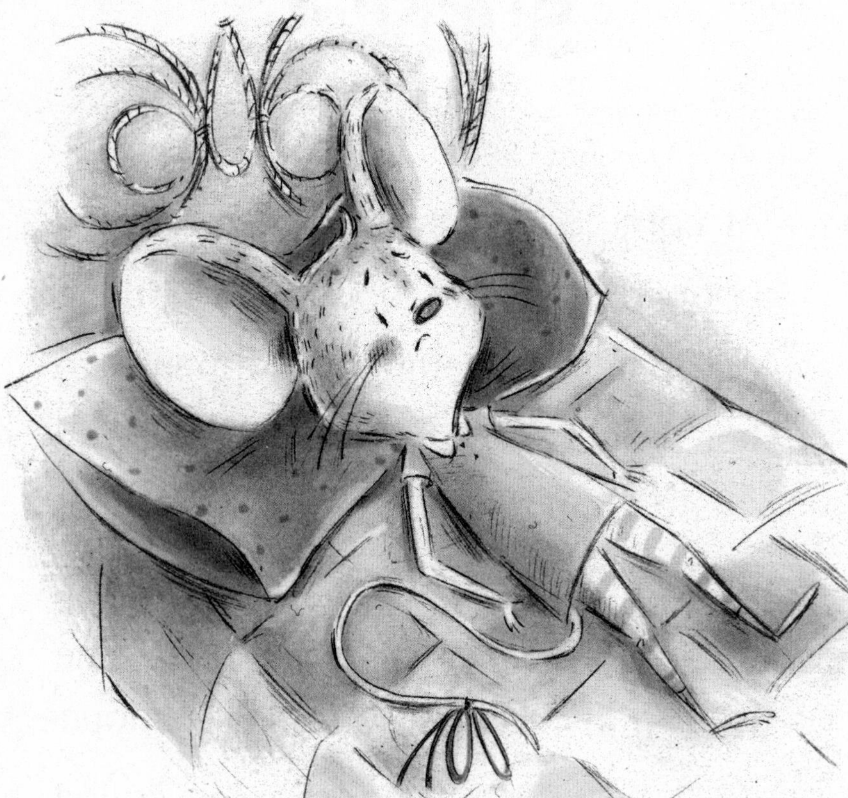

It was a sunny-day scene of Forget-Me-Not Lake. A frog and a snake were racing each other across the lake.

On the shore, one little mouse was waiting for them.

Sophie looked over at her easel. A blank canvas sat there, waiting. She had the painting all worked out. But she didn't actually want to paint it.

She realized she hated the idea of going underwater. Even if mice *could* learn to swim, Sophie didn't want

to. Not anytime soon. She wasn't going to be the Incredible Swimming Mouse, after all. And she still didn't have any exciting mouse facts to include in the presentation.

Sophie moped in her room. At one point she heard her mom's and

Winston's voices downstairs. She figured they were home from the bakery.

A little while later there was another knock at Sophie's bedroom door. "Come in," Sophie called.

The door opened and Hattie and Owen stuck their heads in. Sophie sat up straight. "Oh!" she said, surprised.

"W-what are you two doing here?"

Owen wiggled forward. "We're sorry the swim lesson didn't go so well," he said.

Sophie shrugged. "That's okay," she said gloomily. "Guess I'm just not a swimmer."

Hattie sat down on the end of Sophie's bed. "We want to make it up to you," she said. Then she smiled slyly. "In fact, we have a little surprise for you!"

Sophie couldn't help being curious. "A surprise?" she said. "What *kind* of surprise?"

Hattie and Owen wouldn't tell her.

Instead, Hattie took Sophie's hand. "Just come with us."

So Sophie followed Owen and Hattie outside and toward the town. She didn't ask any more questions—until they turned down the trail that led to Forget-Me-Not Lake.

"Are we going back to the lake?" Sophie asked warily. "Because I don't really want more lessons."

Her friends led her on. "Just come on," said Owen.

They walked farther. They were nearly at the lake.

Sophie added, "Mice might be able to swim. But I'll never be the kind of swimmer

you two are. You'll have more fun without me."

"Sophie," said Hattie, "wait until you see the surprise!"

They walked a little more. Soon they were standing in some tall reeds on the lake shore. Hattie and Owen parted the curtain of reeds at the water's edge.

Floating in the lake was a raft. It was made of twigs tied together with long blades of grass. Resting on top of the raft was a twig paddle.

Sophie noticed it was just the right size for a mouse.

chapter 8

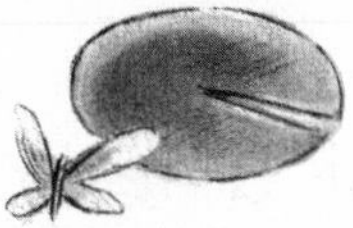

Smells Like Trouble

Right away, Sophie realized what her friends had done—and why.

Owen smiled. "Just because you're not a swimmer—yet—doesn't mean we can't all have fun together in the water."

"Or *on* the water," said Hattie. She gave Sophie a nudge toward the raft. "Go ahead! Try it out!"

Sophie took a hesitant step toward the raft.

"Oh, wait!" Hattie said. "I made this for you—just to be extra safe." Hattie placed a vest made of seed-pods over Sophie's head. There was a dangling string that Hattie tied around Sophie's waist. "It floats!"

Hattie explained. "And it would keep you afloat, too—if needed."

Sophie smiled and carefully stepped onto the raft. She sat down and picked up the paddle. Hattie and Owen gave the raft a gentle push and she was off!

Sophie beamed as she paddled around. Hattie and Owen jumped into the water. They swam around her raft. They splashed water at Sophie. She splashed them back using her paddle.

"Oh, thank you both!" Sophie exclaimed. "This is so much fun! You two are the best friends ever."

Then they had a race. Sophie paddled while her friends swam. Hattie won, but Sophie came in a close second.

"Next time, look out!" Sophie said playfully. "With more practice,

I might get even faster!"

The three friends lost all track of time. They played at the lake for most of the afternoon.

Suddenly, in the middle of a game of water tag, Sophie froze. Her nose and whiskers twitched. She tilted her head back and sniffed the air.

"Do you smell that?" she asked Hattie and Owen.

They sniffed the air too. "Smell what?" asked Owen.

"I don't smell anything," said Hattie.

Sophie sniffed again, just to be sure. "Yep. It's about to rain—a lot."

Hattie's brow wrinkled with worry. "We'd better get home then!" she said uneasily.

The friends tied up the raft along the shore. Then, together, they hurried for home.

"It's a good thing you told us!" Owen said to Sophie as they went. "We could have gotten caught in the rainstorm!"

Sophie stopped in her tracks. "Owen!" she cried. "That's it! A mouse's sense of smell is . . . extraordinary! And it's good for more than just knowing when cakes are ready!"

Hattie and Owen looked confused. But Sophie just smiled proudly as they hurried along. She couldn't wait to tell Winston that she had a great idea for their presentation!

chapter 9
A MOLE'S LIFE

Fun Facts

On Tuesday at school, all the students arrived ready to share their projects with the class. Mrs. Wise called each species up, one at a time, to do their presentation.

Sophie was curious to see what everyone else had done—and surprised to learn many things she did not know about them.

Of course she knew that most birds could fly. "But did you know that bird bones are hollow inside?" Zoe the bluebird said.

Sophie also learned that rabbits' teeth never stop growing. She learned that frogs can breathe through their skin. And she learned that squirrels sometimes forget where they buried their acorns. "Forgotten acorns can grow into oak trees," said Ellie the squirrel. "So you could say that squirrels plant trees!"

Then it was Sophie and Winston's turn to talk about mice. They proudly showed off the poster they'd made together. Sophie had painted some pictures of mice climbing, jumping, balancing, and squeezing through tight spaces. There was even one of a mouse swimming.

"Mice *can* swim," Winston said. "But not all mice like to."

Sophie looked over at Hattie and Owen. They smiled at her.

Then Sophie pointed to the last picture—of a mouse sniffing the air. "Mice have a great sense of smell, and their whiskers can sense changes in temperature—which might be why I feel like I can 'smell' when the rain is coming!"

Sophie smiled. It was a really cool fact that she hadn't even known about herself before they'd done the project.

That night, in her bedroom, Sophie painted a beautiful scene of Forget-Me-Not Lake. In it, she was paddling across the lake on her raft, with Owen and Hattie swimming behind. They were racing, and Sophie was about to win.

Sophie stepped back to admire her work. Her new color, cornflower blue, was the perfect shade for the water.

The End

Here's a peek at the next Adventures of Sophie Mouse book!

"Wheeeeeeee!" Sophie squealed with delight. Her voice echoed off the curved wooden walls of the giant tunnel slide. Sophie slid through the darkness. The slide twisted to the right. Then it turned to the left. Sophie grasped the fern she was sitting on. The slide track spiraled around and down, down, down, until—

Sophie came shooting out of the

bottom end. *Fwomp!* She landed in a soft pile of green leaves.

High above, on a birch branch, Sophie's best friends cheered.

"Whoo-hoo!" cried Hattie Frog.

"Wow!" Owen Snake called out. "That's a long way down!"

Birch Tree Slide was a hollow, twisted branch. It leaned up against the trunk of a huge birch tree. To get to the top of the slide, Sophie, Hattie, and Owen had first climbed way up the tree using its knotholes. Sophie had been excited to go first.

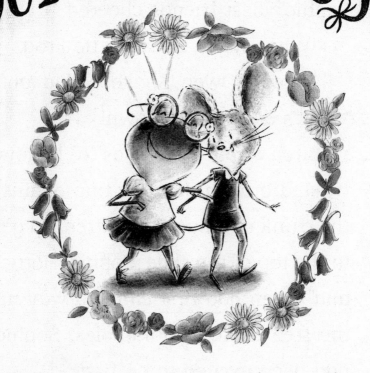